Worth the WAIT

Learning to be More PATIENT

Jasmine Brooke

FOX EYE
PUBLISHING

Monkey found it hard to **WAIT**. She always wanted to do things right **NOW!**

She didn't like **WAITING** in the queue at break.

She wouldn't **WAIT** her turn in swimming lessons.

She never WAITED to ask questions in lessons, and not WAITING could be a problem.

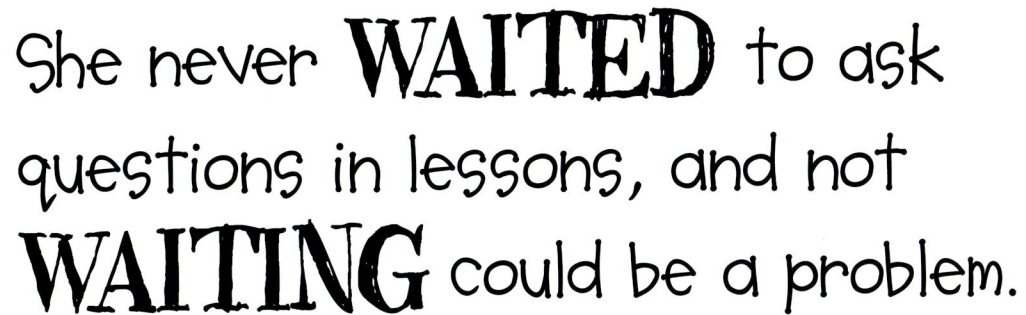

Today, Mrs Tree was teaching the class to bake. Monkey couldn't **WAIT** to start.

Mrs Tree told everyone to weigh their butter, then put it in the bowl. But Monkey couldn't **WAIT** to take her turn with the weighing scales. She just put all her butter in the bowl.

Next, Mrs Tree told everyone to weigh their sugar and put it in the bowl.

Monkey was **IMPATIENT**.

Everyone was taking **TOO LONG** with the weighing scales. So, Monkey didn't weigh her sugar. She just put it all in the bowl.

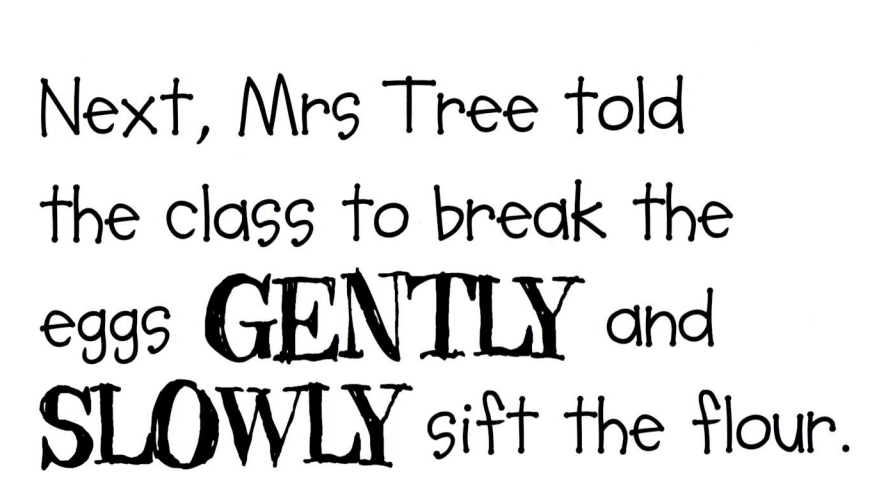

Next, Mrs Tree told the class to break the eggs **GENTLY** and **SLOWLY** sift the flour.

But Monkey wasn't listening. She dropped the eggs straight into the bowl and put all the flour in it, too! Poof!

AT LAST it was time to bake the cakes. Monkey was so excited. She couldn't WAIT for them to cook.

She watched the cakes rise. All except hers. She saw the cakes turn golden. All except hers. Then, Mrs Tree said it was time to take the cakes out of the oven. This time, Monkey **WAITED**. Because everyone's cakes looked delicious – all except hers.

Lion licked his lips. Parrot hopped up and down. Hippo grinned from ear to ear. They couldn't **WAIT** to eat their cakes.

But Monkey wished she had **WAITED** ... waited her turn with the weighing scales, **LISTENED** to Mrs Tree and been more **PATIENT**.

"Don't worry, Monkey," Mrs Tree said kindly. "Shall we try again?" Monkey nodded her head. "Shall we be **PATIENT** and take our time?" Monkey nodded again.

So Mrs Tree and Monkey **PATIENTLY** weighed the butter and the sugar.

They **SLOWLY** sifted the flour and **GENTLY** added the eggs. Then they …

... **WAITED** for the cake to cook, rise and turn golden. Monkey licked her lips.

"Now," said Mrs Tree, "wasn't that worth the wait?" "Mmmm," Monkey agreed, and ate her cake.

Monkey had learnt to **LISTEN** and be **PATIENT**, because some things were worth **WAITING** for. Yum!

Words and feelings

Monkey felt impatient in this story and that made things go wrong.

PATIENT WAIT

SLOWLY

There are a lot of words to do with being patient and being impatient in this book. Can you remember all of them?

IMPATIENT

WAITING

Let's talk about behaviour

This series helps children to understand and manage difficult emotions and behaviours. The animal characters in the series have been created to show human behaviour that is often seen in young children, and which they may find difficult to manage.

Worth the Wait

The story in this book examines issues around being patient. It looks at how being impatient can make things go wrong and lead to disappointment.

The book is designed to show young children how they can manage their behaviour and learn to be patient.

How to use this book

You can read this book with one child or a group of children. The book can be used to begin a discussion around complex behaviour such as managing impatience.

The book is also a reading aid, with enlarged and repeated words to help children to develop their reading skills.

How to read the story

Before beginning the story, ensure that the children you are reading to are relaxed and focused.

Take time to look at the enlarged words and the illustrations, and discuss what this book might be about before reading the story.

New words can be tricky for young children to approach. Sounding them out first, slowly and repeatedly, can help children to learn the words and become familiar with them.

How to discuss the story

When you have finished reading the story, use these questions and discussion points to examine the theme of the story with children and explore the emotions and behaviours within it:

- What do you think the story was about? Have you been in a situation in which you found it hard to be patient? What was that situation? For example, did you rush through a project instead of taking your time? Encourage the children to talk about their experiences.
- Talk about ways that people can cope with wanting things quickly. For example, take deep breaths and remind yourself that waiting for something is worth it. Talk to the children about what tools they think might work for them and why.
- Discuss the problems that result from not being patient. Explain that Monkey rushed in the story, and that caused trouble for her.
- Talk about why it is important to be patient and take your time when carrying out a task. Discuss the value of doing so.

Titles in the series

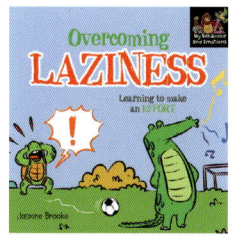 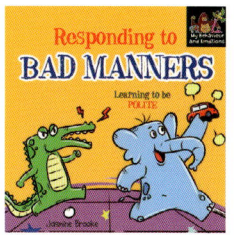 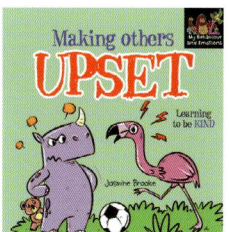 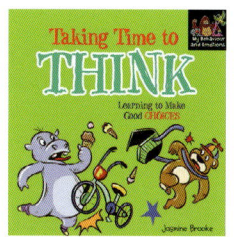 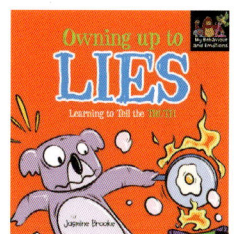

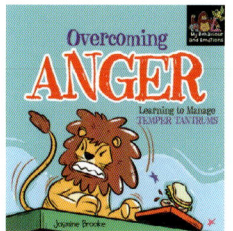 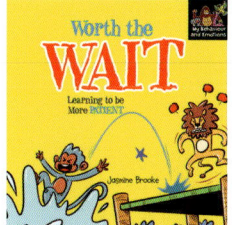 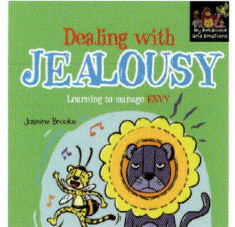  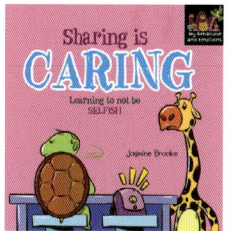

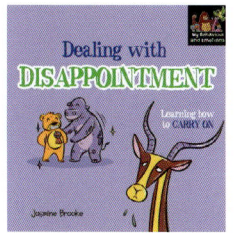 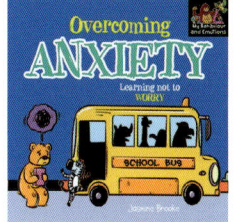 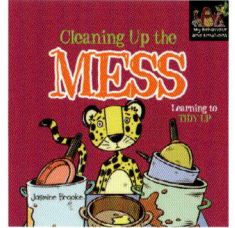  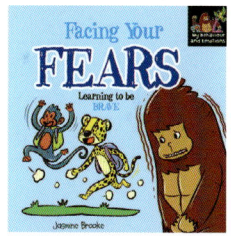

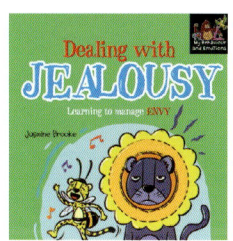 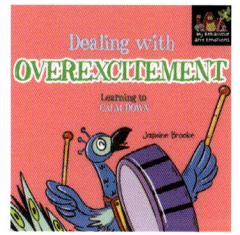 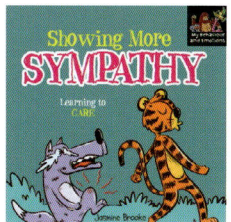 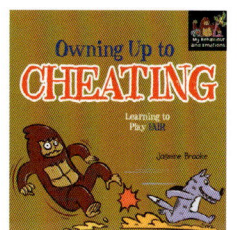 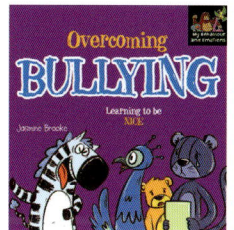

First published in 2023 by Fox Eye Publishing
Unit 31, Vulcan House Business Centre,
Vulcan Road, Leicester, LE5 3EF
www.foxeyepublishing.com

Copyright © 2023 Fox Eye Publishing
All rights reserved. No portion of this book may be reproduced in any form without permission from the publisher, except as permitted by U.K. copyright law.

Author: Jasmine Brooke
Art director: Paul Phillips
Cover designer: Emma Bailey & Salma Thadha
Editor: Jenny Rush

All illustrations by Novel

ISBN 978-1-80445-288-2

A catalogue record for this book is available from the British Library

Printed in China